ANTHONY BROW

Our Girl

For Martha and Juliet

PICTURE CORGI
UK | USA | Canada | Ireland | Australia | India | New Zealand | South Africa
Picture Corgi is part of the Penguin Random House group of companies
whose addresses can be found at global.penguinrandomhouse.com.

www.penguin.co.uk www.puffin.co.uk www.ladybird.co.uk

First published by Doubleday 2020
This paperback edition published 2021
001

Printed in China

The authorized representative in the EEA is Penguin Random House Ireland,
Morrison Chambers, 32 Nassau Street, Dublin D02 YH68

A CIP catalogue record for this book is available
from the British Library

ISBN: 978-0-552-57760-1

All correspondence to: Picture Corgi, Penguin Random House Children's
One Embassy Gardens, 8 Viaduct Gardens, London SW11 7BW

ANTHONY BROWNE

Our Girl

PICTURE CORGI

She's lovely, our girl.

Our girl loves animals . . .

(Even mice!)

She's a great goalie

and a brilliant swimmer.

She makes fantastic drawings

and she's great at dressing up.

She's lovely, our girl.

Sometimes she speaks quietly

and sometimes she shouts

VERY LOUDLY!

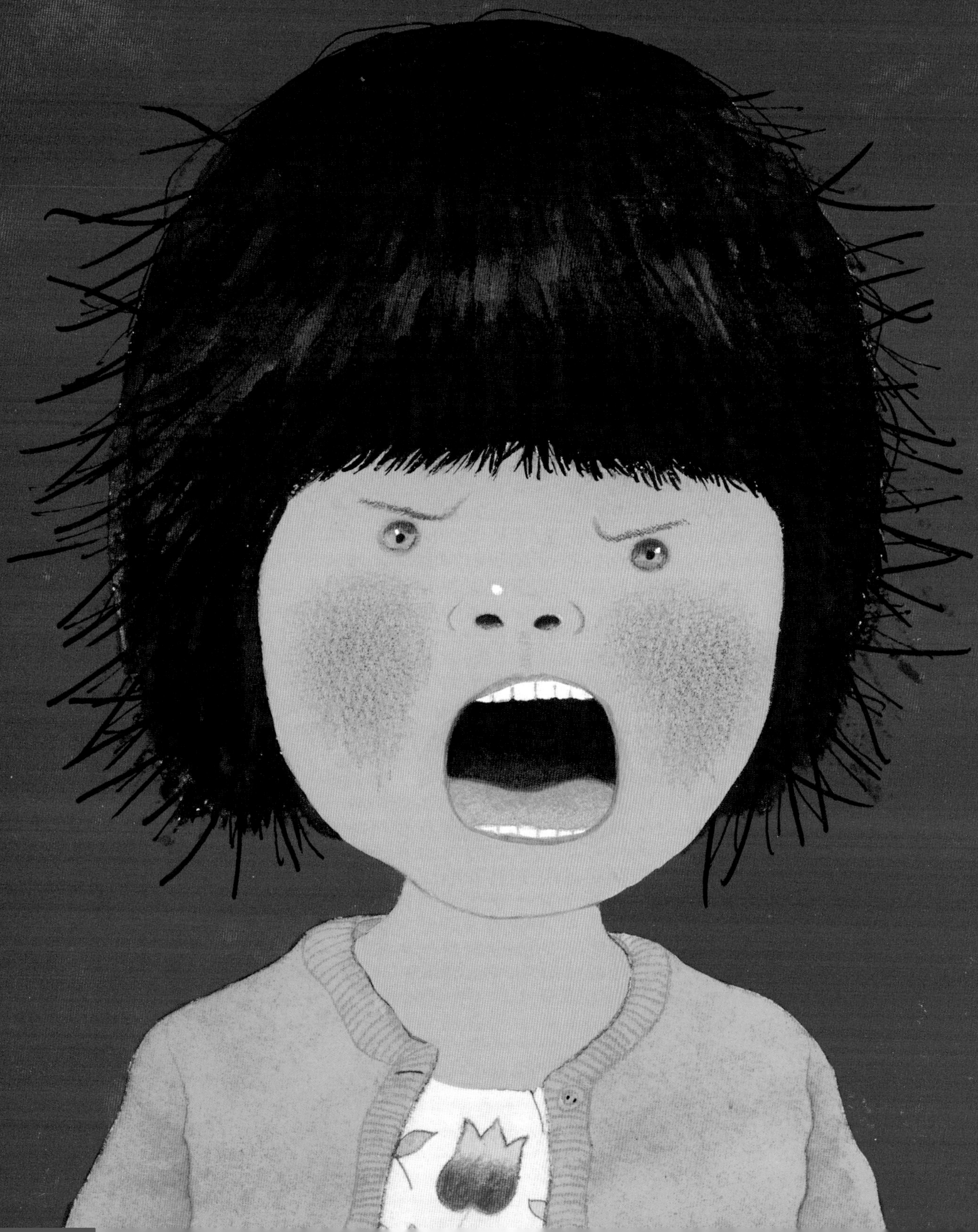

She can climb like a panda

and jump like a frog!

She's as grand as a lady

and as cheeky as a monkey.

But she's lovely, our girl.

She's a builder

and a doctor.

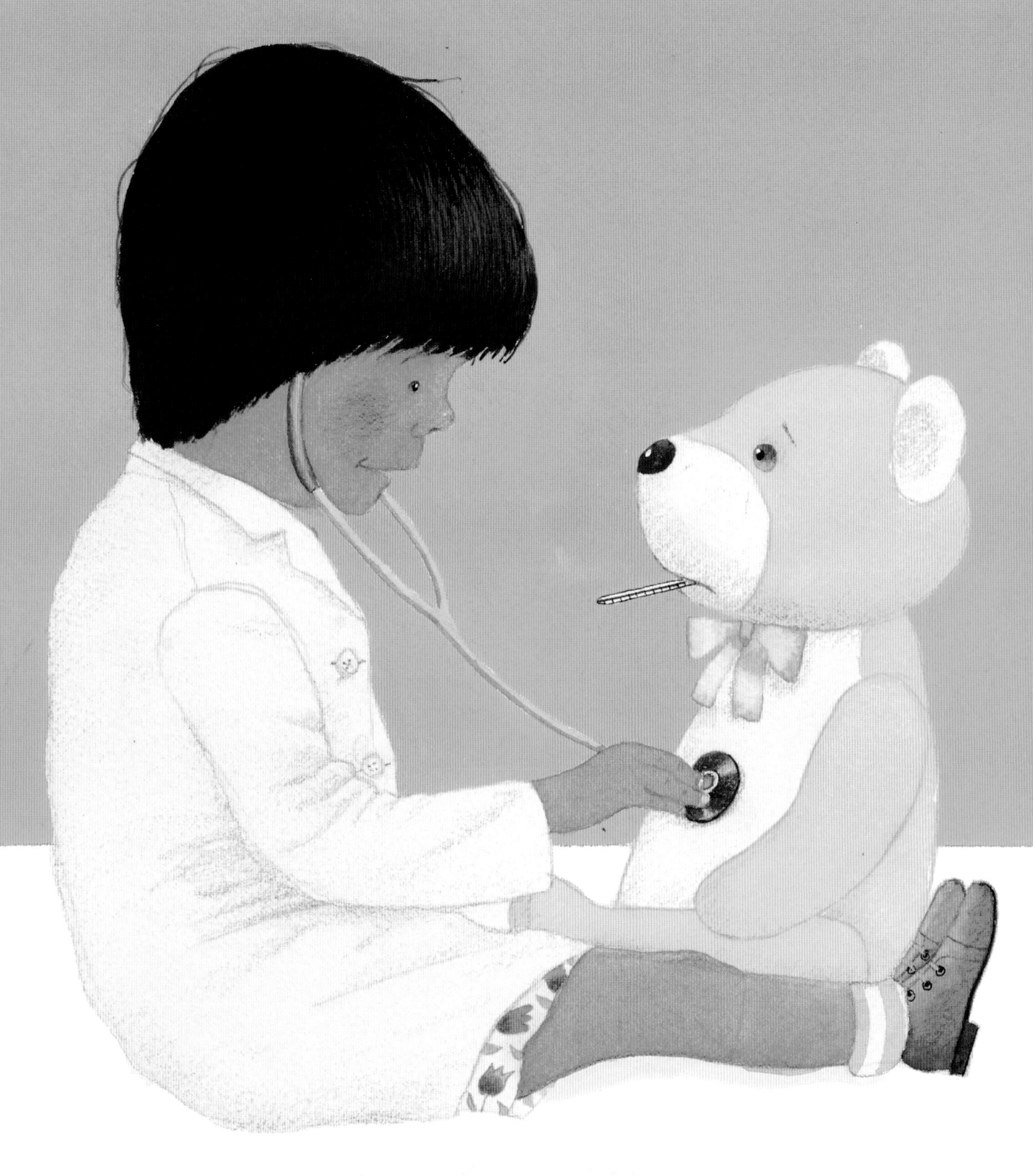

She can be as busy as a bee

or as sleepy as a dog.

Sometimes we fight . . .

but then she gives me
a beautiful smile!

You are really,
really lovely,
our girl.

And guess what?

WE
LOVE
YOU!

(And we always will.)